DRAGONS OF THE PRIME
POEMS ABOUT DINOSAURS

for Joyce Junkin, 1934–2018

THE EMMA PRESS

First published in the UK in 2019 by the Emma Press Ltd.

Poems © individual copyright holders 2019
Selection © Richard O'Brien 2019
Notes © Will Tattersdill 2019
Illustrations and design © Emma Dai'an Wright 2019

ISBN 978-1-912915-05-7

A CIP catalogue record of this book is available
 from the British Library.

Printed and bound in the EU by Pulsio, Paris.

The Emma Press
theemmapress.com
hello@theemmapress.com
Jewellery Quarter, Birmingham, UK

Supported using public funding by
**ARTS COUNCIL
ENGLAND**

DRAGONS OF THE PRIME
POEMS ABOUT
DINOSAURS

Edited by Richard O'Brien

With notes by Will Tattersdill
Illustrated by Emma Dai'an Wright

INTRODUCTION

When I was a kid, I loved dinosaurs. While my mum went to work, I spent a lot of time at my nan's house, reading magazines about dinosaurs over her shoulder and learning their long, complicated Latin names. She used to joke that this was how I learnt to read, and that might be true. But dinosaurs definitely inspired my imagination. No one alive today has ever seen a dinosaur, and this means that everything we know about them is the result of people making up stories.

Scientists make up stories, when they piece together the bones they find and use that evidence to imagine what they might have looked like, how they might have moved. Film-makers do the same, using animatronic models to bring these extinct beasts to life in movies like *Jurassic World* or the TV show *Walking With Dinosaurs*. And the stories we tell about them are changing all the time because of new discoveries: nowadays we're just as likely to picture dinosaurs with brightly-coloured feathers as with leathery scales, and some new research suggests that dinosaurs didn't even roar. Instead, they might have growled like crocodiles, or even honked like a goose!

In this anthology, a range of poets have written their own responses to dinosaurs and the powerful effect they have on our imaginations. Some of the poems are extremely scientifically accurate, while others are more fantastical. The poets have thought about dinosaurs as they existed in their own time – the Mesozoic era – and about how it feels to brush away the dirt and discover their enigmatic fossils in the present day. Lots of different dinosaurs star in their own poems across the course of the book, so I hope every reader will find something about their own favourite. And if they're not featured here, there are also some fun writing exercises in the final pages which encourage you to explore your own Cretaceous creativity.

I think dinosaurs are a great subject for poetry because they make us think about what another world was like: our own Earth, but very long ago. They also make us think about language: saying all those difficult names, when all the animals you've seen in real life are called things like 'pig' and 'dog' and 'duck', is almost like using a magic summoning spell.

I never became a palaeontologist, like I wanted to do when I was little (I'm not very good at hard physical work, and I know I'd probably just end up breaking something important with a spade). But I did become a writer. Those dinosaur days – building balsa wood models, taking trips to see Dippy at the Natural History Museum – helped to awake my imagination, and I think the same is true for kids all over. My nan didn't get to see this book, but I think she would have liked it. I hope you like it too, and that reading these poems reminds you what amazing stories are out there beneath the soil, in the pre-history of the earth.

Richard O'Brien

APRIL 2019

A NOTE ON THE NOTES

Poets might choose to repeat myths or ideas about dinosaurs which are out-of-date in scientific terms because they tell a better story, but all good palaeontologists have to sift through what they find very carefully...

That's why we asked Will Tattersdill, a writer who studies the different ways scientists and artists present dinosaurs to the public, to write some factual notes that sit alongside the poems. Will's notes point out where the writing gets particularly creative and help you to think critically about the line between fact and fiction.

A NOTE ON NAMES

All animals known to scientists, living or dead, have a two-part name made up of a genus (a larger group, like felines) and a species (a smaller group, like cats), creating something like *Felis catus*. Scientific convention means that these names often come from Latin and Greek, and are always written in *italics*.

These scientific names help researchers to be as precise as possible when talking about specimens, but it would make the poems pretty hard to read if we insisted on using italics and only calling the dinosaurs by their scientific names when writing about dinosaurs more informally. So, we decided to print their names in normal writing in the poems and use the full scientific versions in Will's notes.

CONTENTS

BONUS BITS

WHO MADE THIS BOOK?

DINOSAURS WALKED HERE

Elli Woollard

Dinosaurs walked here once.
Here, right here, on the site of this street,
they'd stamp along, and the slabs of their feet
were as wide as a car, crushing, crashing
a road through the reeds. Then, striding and splashing,
they'd thud in the mud of the deep green pool,
and they'd clomp in the swamp under new-forged skies
where now the cold grey concrete lies.
Or they'd stop, by the shop where we go for our snacks,
and with mouths gaping wide they'd commence their attacks.
Claw-jaw clash as they leapt on their prey,
who'd go desperately darting and dashing away.
But the beasts who were bigger would launch on their lunch
with a roar and a rip and lash-slash crunch.

Then perhaps where that cat's lying curled, they would sleep,
each of their bodies a truck-wide heap.
And see, on that building site, right over there,
their necks were cranes that rose in the air,
as tower block-tall they stood and sang
their ageless song, till the whole earth rang
with their voices, strong and clear and loud.
Lords of the land, they were, and proud
as they roamed their timeless realm. No more.
All there is now is the thunderous roar
of indifferent traffic, speeding on by.
The reeds are gone. The swamp is dry,
leaving only a puddle on paving stones.
Nothing remains. Not even bones.
But dinosaurs walked here,
once.

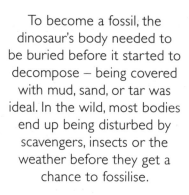

To become a fossil, the dinosaur's body needed to be buried before it started to decompose – being covered with mud, sand, or tar was ideal. In the wild, most bodies end up being disturbed by scavengers, insects or the weather before they get a chance to fossilise.

Only a fraction the dinosaurs that ever lived became really great fossils and – of course – only a fraction of *these* survive in the Earth's crust to be found millennia later. For every story we know about the dinosaurs, there are thousands we will never know.

THE DINOSAUR ALPHABET

Harry Man

Ankylosaurus is dressed in armour,
Baryonyx likes his fish,
Coelophysis is quick to strike but
Dacentrurus has to swish.

Edmontosaurus is big and scary.
Fruitadens is small and wary.
Gorgosaurus chomps her meat.
Hadrosaurus nibbles leaves.

Iguanodon has one big thumb.
Jinzhousaurus likes to run.
Kritosaurus smells the best.
Limaysaurus has ooOo0o0ooOOoonnnnnnnnne
            looO00oooonnnnnnnnnnnnnnnnnnnng neck.

Megalosaurus is always first.
Noasaurus farts and burps.
Oviraptors steal your eggs.
Patagotitan stomps about on big BIG BIG BIG LEGS!

sssssshhhhhhh!

Quaesitosaurus can hear us too!

Regnosaurus is too cool for school.

Stegosaurus has spines that are big and tough.

T. rex wants to eat you up!

Utahraptor smooths his crest.

Velociraptor patrols the nest.

Wulagasaurus quacks like a duck.

Xenoceratops has three horns, and a fourth – just for luck.

Yinlong was an ancient lizard as big as you!

Zephyrosaurus likes to fly, *Please Zephyrosaurus, can we fly too?*

Megalosaurus was the first dinosaur to be named. In fact, it was named before the word 'dinosaur' had even been invented! This was back in 1824, the same year as Beethoven's famous ninth symphony was first performed.

Yinlong was discovered in China, and its name means 'hidden dragon'. Have a look at Gita Raleigh's poem on page 60 for more on Chinese dinosaurs.

TINY
(Junornis huoi)

Ruth Wiggins

Was that me? Yes!
Did you see?

Me! dashing round
the playing field.

Golden and bright
a thing of light

a bounding, joy
of spring-sprung thing.

Flying across
the hockey pitch, just me!

HOO-EE!
Who needs the wind?

See me dodge and weave.
See the ribbon

of the finish line, stream
like a tail

from me, all me.
See my wings?

Did you blink?
Well you missed me.

Junornis was about the size of a
little bird. This is because it was
a little bird, bounding round the
skies of Inner Mongolia just like
a modern skylark and just like
the lines of this poem.

A BABY DIPLODOCUS PRAYS

John Kitchen

wanna be a bludgeoner
an awfully gruesome guy
wanna put my foot down
make archaeopteryx cry

wanna be the eardrum splitter
wanna be fierce and brave
wanna be a clifftop diver
cause a tidal wave

wanna shmooze in volcanic pools
gulp and guzzle and splash
the bone cruncher the flesh muncher
wanna be Mister Flash

wanna trounce tyrannosaur
want the brontosaur to shake
wanna stick it to the stegosaur

watch velociraptor quake

let me slurp
let me stomp
let me slaver
let me chomp
let me live in a dank dark den

that's it
I think

so thank you, Lord amen

The *Quetzalcoatlus* was a huge pterosaur. Its wingspan was around 10 metres, roughly the same as five grownups in massive hats lying end to end.

The name *Maiasaura* means 'good mother lizard'. It got this name because it was the first dinosaur shown to have looked after its babies. Fossils of a *Maiasaura* nesting colony were discovered in the late 1970s.

A PRAYER AT BEDTIME

Finlay Worrallo

My child,

May you grow to fly like a pterodactyl,
and run like a gallimimus.
May you charge at obstacles like a furious triceratops,
and reach for the sky like a brachiosaurus.
May your triumphs ring out like a hadrosaur call,
and shake the ground like seismosaurus feet.
May you dive as deep as a liopleurodon,
and soar as high as a quetzalcoatlus.
May you and your friends move as one
like a velociraptor pack.
May you fight like a stegosaurus,
feast like a T. rex,
and love like a maiasaura.

And may no asteroid ever stop you.

THE JIGSAURUS PUZZLE

Cat Weatherill

Dinosaur Valley State Park, Texas, USA
1 April 2018

A statement from expedition leader Angus Digger–Down,
Professor of Palaeontology, Fossil College, Cambridge, UK.

'Deep in the ground
My team has found
The bones of a mighty Jigsaurus

The question now
Is exactly how
To deal with the problem before us

There are countless bits
Nothing fits
I'm not quite sure what to do

There's no picture to follow
We're leaving tomorrow
And nobody brought any glue.'

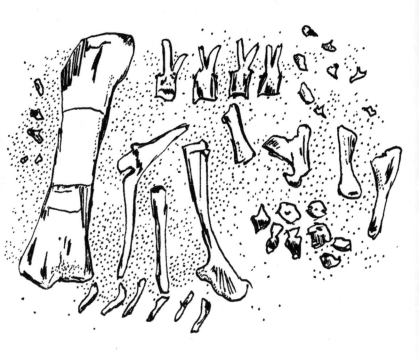

When's the best time to dig up dinosaurs? In the summer! If you'd like to give it a go, remember to take plenty of plaster to keep the bones safe while you helicopter them off to your museum.

Then you can spend winter in the basement trying to fit them all together. Of course, if you're lucky enough to find something small, this will all be much easier...

MY GRANDDAD, THE DINOSAUR

Lorraine Mariner

My granddad is trying
to text my mum
to tell her what time
the train we're on

will arrive at the station.
We've been visiting
the Natural History Museum,
our favourite place.

'I'm all fingers and thumbs,'
my granddad grumbles,
'The words are spelt wrong
and when I press send

nothing happens!
I'm old and out of date,
I'm such a dinosaur,
I should be on display!'

What can Granddad mean?
The dinosaur gallery
is the coolest place to be
and my granddad knows more

about dinosaurs than my teacher –
than Google even!
'Granddad, you're not extinct,'
I tell him, 'You've got me

to help you with computers.
Give me that phone,
I'll text Mum, tell me some more
about the Microraptor.'

The famous Natural History
Museum in London first opened
in 1881. If you look closely at the
outside of the building you will see
the pterosaur gargoyles! For more
on the museum, have a look at John
Canfield's poem on page 47.

WING FINGER

Valerie Valente

Today, I saw the bones of a pterodactylus.
He was laid neatly in a case at the History Museum.
His head was long,
with a beak like a stork.
   I wondered if he'd ever done some pre-historic fishing.
He had funny, little stick legs
and three fingers on his hands.
   I imagined him swooping above all our heads.
   His bat-like wings would stretch so wide as he glided.
   His shrill cries terrifying all the other girls from school.
   They'd squeal in panic,
   breathless with fear,
   as they ducked behind Miss Daniels.
   But our teacher would be equally as frightened –
   hair frantically escaping from the tight knot of her bun.
   All the while, I would simply watch in wonder
   just to witness such a creature;
   a reptile in flight.
Isn't it funny that walking dinosaurs truly had feathers,
but the soaring pterodactylus just wore his lizard skin?
His fossilized footprints teach us
that he would walk upon all fours,
like a lumbering ape,
when he landed.

The boys might run to catch him,
but he'd soon warn them off;
squawking and slashing his beak like a sword.
They'd all be wise to leave him be
if they valued their own fingers.
I'd observe him from a distance,
simply amazed by his every small movement.
We'd have an understanding,
he and I.
He'd clatter upon the polished floors;
unsteady.
And I'm sure he'd be real hungry.
But, being without fish,
I'd simply have to offer
the gummy sweets
I'd crammed into my coat pockets
instead.

There are a few million
dinosaurs left – in fact, you
might have seen one today!
Birds, descendants of a group
of dinosaurs called theropods,
are all around us.

DINOSAUR SONNET

Camille Gagnier

Dad sometimes calls the car a dinosaur,
but says that real dinosaurs have not been
around since grandpa was a kid, and laughs.
He is a real goof. If there are no
dinosaurs on the entire earth, then
why do people always talk about them?
In New York they have great dinosaur bones.
We do not know what skin they wore when they
were living. If we go extinct, how will
the scientists put our bones back together?
Octopi taste like chicken, but they are much
smarter than chickens. When the oceans grow
high, the octopi will study our
fossils by the wet ruins of Coney
Island. In the underwater towers
of Manhattan, side by side with our old
T. rex, they will imagine my favourite
foods, my bad dreams, the colour of my feet.

ONE DAY

Richard O'Brien

I could have been a triceratops one day,
with a ridge on my head,
the hint of a horn:
you can see it on my skull if you look closely.

Big, high eyes. One day,
I might have become a strong swimmer:
short legs can grow
into paddling feet. Not mine, though.

New hatchlings have soft bones. One day
you'll find this out. You'll find
me, in the belly of

a hairy creature
that got hungry one day,
no bigger than a badger.

Evolution is a weird idea to think about: everything alive is related – and changing all the time. In this poem, the poet imagines evolution to be happening very quickly, although in real life it takes millions of years.

For more on the mammals which survived the dinosaurs, see Jeremy Wikeley's poem on page 89.

WATCHING *THE LAND BEFORE TIME* WITH MUM

Wye Haze

She smoothed the blanket and passed me the bowl of popcorn
Right from the start, I could tell she was going to cry.
It's the music, she said, when I asked her why.

When Littlefoot was born, she started to cry. I asked her why
You'll see when you grow up, she sniffed, and passed me the
    popcorn.
Sometimes I don't understand what makes her cry.

Then you-know-what happened! I tried my best not to cry.
Mum hugged me tight. I didn't ask why.
She looked at the empty bowl, pressed pause, and said
    More popcorn?

The warm salty popcorn came and I started to cry.
    Mum smiled. She didn't ask why.

People who make films have always been obsessed with dinosaurs. In 1914, one of the very first animated films featured Gertie, a *Brontosaurus*, drinking an entire lake!

Ever since then, each time film technology becomes more advanced, it's never too long before dinosaurs are back on the big screens...

A REAL LIVE FOSSIL

Rachael M Nicholas

What was it like, back at the beginning of you?

Before dust,
before the fire finished time's slow work,
before the museum,
before we pieced you together, all of your puzzle-parts,
before we named you, brand new: *swift-footed lizard.*

What was it like, back before I found you?
And before the days before I found you?
Before the boulder cracked like an egg
and spilled your secrets.

What was it like before that?
Before the glacier scooped you up
and carried you along,
all those years and miles away.

Were you waiting?

Before you stripped down to bare bones,
before you laid down on the ground for good,
before your

very

      last

           day.

And all the days before that – what were they like?

Back at the beginning of you,
when you first stepped, unsteady,
out on to the earth?

Mignon Talbot discovered
the only known fossils of
the *Podokesaurus* ('swift-
footed lizard') in 1910.

On making the discovery she
called out to her sister: '... come
quick, I have found a real live
fossil!' Sadly, the museum that
housed the specimen burned
down in 1917.

THIEF

Richard O'Brien

Know this, you men who chipped away
the dirt: those were my eggs. My brood.
I loved them, but I could not stay.
Know this, human who chipped away
my motherhood, my care, the day
you framed those fragments as my food,
know this: though time has stripped away
my name, these are my eggs. My brood.

This poem is about an appalling injustice and a wrongful accusation! There's a dinosaur called *Oviraptor* whose name literally means 'egg thief', because the person who discovered it (in 1924) noticed that it was near a large nest and drew some conclusions.

We've since learned that this dinosaur wasn't stealing the eggs after all, but looking after them. The rules of science forbid a name change in situations like this (see Jane Frank's poem on page 85 for another example of this problem), so we have to continue to accuse this innocent beast of theft and murder every time we say its name. Sorry, *Oviraptor*!

DAWN OF THE DINOSAUR

Emma Rose Millar

The prehistoric ocean was full of wondrous sights:
sponges, coral, jellyfish and curly ammonites.
But all of this was not enough for fish who found it drab,
they wanted out – to live on land, where everything seemed fab.
They grew a spiny backbone, a separate head and tail,
then grew some grew legs, and left the sea, and walked out on the shale.
These tetrapods all lurched and reeled, and stumbled on all fours,
and on each leg grew seven toes and seven spiky claws.
They colonised the bog land, the fen, the swamp, the marsh,
and found that though the sea was dull, dry land was twice as harsh.

Forty million years went by: new creatures roamed the land,
but they laid their eggs in water, and stayed close to the sand.
They still have some descendants: salamanders, toads and frogs,
who start with gills and have cold blood, and live in streams and bogs.

Next came prehistoric turtles, crocodiles and snakes –
because their skin was dry and tough they ventured from the lakes.

Among this group of reptiles, with semi-porous eggs,
were hardy beasts called archosaurs who walked on just two legs.
From these Triassic archosaurs, the dinosaurs were spawned:
the day of Herrersauruses and Eoraptors dawned.
And all because of lobe-finned fish who found the ocean bland,
and grew some legs so they could seek adventures on the land.

HOW BIG IS A DINOSAUR EGG?

Helen Clare

Just how big is a dinosaur egg?
Is it bigger than a nutmeg?
As big as a potato?
As big as a tomato?
As big as a plate – oh?!

Just how tall is a dinosaur egg?
Is it taller than your leg?
As tall as a street light?
Is it higher than the Dolomites?
Higher than the flight
of a runaway kite?

Just how heavy is a dinosaur egg?
Is it as heavy as a beer keg?
As heavy as my chubby cat,
as heavy as a leaden hat?
As heavy as a falling acrobat
going splat?
Splat!

Just how wide is a dinosaur egg?
Is it wide as Winnipeg?
Is it wide as your settee?
Wide as the beaches in Torquay?
Wider than a very wide wide-screen tv?

Tell me now, don't make me beg:
just how big is a dinosaur egg?

The rocks in the Dolomites
(a mountain range in Italy)
are mostly Triassic in age.
So there's a good chance of
finding an early dinosaur if
you happen to be passing
through!

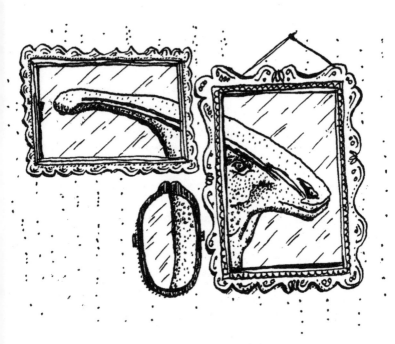

Parasaurolophus was a hadrosaurid, and is sometimes called a 'duckbilled dinosaur'. Though its skull has a beaky appearance, in life it would have been covered in flesh and skin – not like a duck at all.

Because only some bits of dinosaurs (usually bones) are preserved in fossils, we still have loads of questions about how they lived. How much would you be able to guess about what your great-great-great-grandmother looked like if you only had her skeleton?

PARASAUROLOPHUS

Richard O'Brien

Parasauro... low-fuss.
Parasauro... chill.
Parasauro—lizard
with a bird-like bill.

Parasauro—peaceful.
Para—so relaxed.
Running on two legs
when bigger beasts attack.

Parasauro—long crest,
curving like a horn.
Parasauro—long before
we all were born:

Parasauro—guesswork.
Scientists debate:
was it what they waggled
to attract a mate?

Was it like a snorkel,
bobbing in a pool?
Did it fire jets
of blazing chemicals?

Was it like 'Hands up'
In Parasauro—school?
Did it help to move the head?
Or did it just look cool?

Parasauro—secrets.
Parasauro—shtum.
Parasauro—*if we say,*
you'll all want one.

Parasauro—music,
calling to the herd.
Can't be parasauro—certain,
but that's what we've heard.

Parasauro—listen.
Hear its hollow call
in the Parasauro—forest
rise, then fall.

IGUANODON'T

Richard O'Brien

Iguanodon't want to discuss it.
Iguanodon't get in my space.
Iguanodon't see why you don't understand:
it's as plain as the nose on your face.

Iguanodon't you know what happened?
Iguanodon't act like you don't.
The scientists thought my thumb-bone was my nose.
Did they think that my back was my front?

Iguanodon't worry, don't worry.
Iguanodon't give them the time.
Iguanodon't let them define you.
Their words can't do that. Nor can mine.

Famous early reconstructions
of pointy-thumbed *Iguanodon*
mistook the spike for a sort
of rhino horn. But go easy on
them: they were working from
only a few fossils, and the bone
beds were extremely messy!

FORMERLY MR IGUANODON,
LATELY OF THE ISLE OF WIGHT

Lesley Sharpe

I am now Mantellisaurus, my new name.
In the beginning I wasn't put together
with glue. I grew. I was once as small as you
though now you could dismantle all
my pieces, lay them out on the ground,
just as they were when they found me.
That was 1915. I'd been under earth
for more than a hundred million years,
and I might still be there if they hadn't
kept digging, brushing and dusting off,
numbering, labelling, packing in crates
and boxes all my parts, rebuilt me.
See how they set my ribs in space again,
filled them with the cavity of air,
under rib and inner pelvis all shining,
polished and unfleshed in this museum.
My reptile armour is off.
I am all air and space, a great corset –
though look at my three-pronged feet,
their black fossil talons. Imagine me in my prime.

I am one of the most complete dinosaurs
ever found. Is there anything you'd like to know?
I take the long view. Why not? What's the rush?
I still have most of my teeth –
not bad for my age. All these bones –
I am a walking xylophone.
I'm beautiful, if symmetry
and engineering are a kind of beauty.
My heel is upright, bronzed as old wood;
the pieces of my tail are an easy puzzle
though I think the last one is missing.
My elbow is a complex junction of bones
just like yours, my hands shaped round
an invisible football – four fingers and a short claw,
five linked bones for each finger, like you.

Iguanodon means 'iguana tooth', because the teeth of this animal (which were the first part of it found) resembled those of a massive iguana.

Gideon Mantell, the scientist who named *Iguanodon*, thought it would have been around 18 metres long (the length of a normal city bus with a very small car tucked behind it).

We now think it was more like 10 metres (the length of about five queen-size beds).

VELOCIRAPTORS

Rob Walton

velociraptors were not voluptuous
some say they climbed trees, mostly coniferous

their name is said to mean swift seizer,
nifty plunderer, lightning geezer

they roamed this planet in times cretaceous
to little reptiles they were vexatious

with a sickle-shaped claw on the second toe
the prey was hooked: nowhere to go

the size of a small child, ideal for show-and-tell
note the strange mark where your teacher fell

Some recent movies have shown *Velociraptors* as being big enough to take on humans. The real-life things were the size of turkeys, although you still wouldn't have wanted to start a fight with them.

KRONOSAURUS

Cheryl Pearson

See the bones hung from the roof
of the cool hall, how they look
like the ribs of a boat. The hull
and keel, the long body tapered

to a point. A million years have
stripped it to its struts. Once,
a dip in the ocean might have brought
you face to face – imagine that!

Thirty feet of brute strength
and teeth, faster than a shark,
snap snap snapping at your heels
in dark water. Doesn't that give you pause

for thought? It's quite enough to make me
glad of giant squid, and jellyfish, and even
Jaws. I'd rather share the sea with *them*
than a single hungry pliosaur…

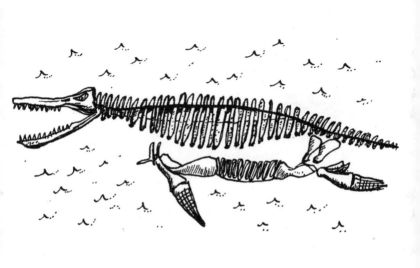

ORNITHOCHEIRUS –
GIANT OF THE SKIES

Rebecca Rouillard

Ornithocheirus – giant of the skies,
lofty patriarch of a remnant few;
raise your crest, spread your ancient wings and rise.

You've a wingspan of remarkable size,
you're the terror of the pterosaur crew;
Ornithocheirus – giant of the skies.

An odd-shaped snout and protuberant eyes,
you're a duck-billed flapper, cruising the blue.
Raise your crest, spread your ancient wings and rise.

Majestic wheeler coasting thermal highs,
(did you ever suspect an ill wind blew?)
Ornithocheirus – giant of the skies.

The sun sinks, no use raging, you are wise,
alone, with a solemn dignity, you
raise your crest, spread your ancient wings and rise.

The meteor looms, light dwindles and dies,
time calls your name out for your final cue:
Ornithocheirus – giant of the skies,
raise your crest, and for one last flight – arise.

Here we meet the famous Chicxulub asteroid, often thought to have destroyed the dinosaurs (and lots of other animals like this *Ornithocheirus*) when it hit what is now Mexico at the end of the Cretaceous period.

Whilst the asteroid impact would not have been fun, there is evidence that it was only one of the things which finished the non-bird dinosaurs off – a huge volcanic eruption in what is now India, for example, is also partly responsible.

HOW TO BE A FUSED LIZARD
(Ankylosaurus)

Jon Stone

Self-assemble at ground level,
sturdy as an anvil so you don't unravel.
Keep very low, and let the teeth of hostiles
go glancing off your back in red hot snarls.
Shrug off bruises, grazes, nicks and minor burns
till extra bones start sprouting from your shoulderbones,
thick and gnarled, cobbled, arcing, flared and broad,
multiplying down your spine, a flowerbed
of warty plates that knit themselves together
under a tarpaulin of living leather.
Now you're hauling such a claw-proof crust,
a bristling, umbo-studded fortress-nest,
stay low, and let your bad moods gather in
the wrecking ball you're pulling on a chain.
It's dented, hovering – a heavy, ugly tool.
Wear it as your tail.

Glossary.

Tarpaulin: a strong sheet of water-resistant material (eg. tarred canvas or plastic) stretched and tied down over cargo for protection.

Umbo (also called 'shield boss'): a round piece of material at the centre of a shield, made for deflecting blows, or as an ornament.

HOW TO BE A SPIKED LIZARD
(Kentrosaurus)

Jon Stone

Dress very crisply, in the latest fashion.
Practise the art of the pointed observation.
Whenever someone hurts you, get revenge.
Be sharp-tongued and sharp-elbowed wherever you range.
The thorns will spring from your body's toughest knots:
crooked kukris, cleavers, sabres – a veritable dreadnought's
feast of prongs, but nastier, all of them yours.
You'll have to bend down under this rack of skewers,
and your head will grow narrow as you come to peer
out from your spiny forest to softly glower,
leaning to tear at the grass and chew
while others learn to steer clear of you.

Glossary.

Kukri: a large curved knife, used in Nepal as a tool
and a weapon.

Dreadnought: a large battleship armed with many
heavy-calibre guns.

TERRIBLE LIZARD

John Canfield

The man who called them *Dinosaurs*
named them in 1842 –
he coined the term from Greek, of course:
Sauros means Lizard, grafted to

Deinos – that's something terrible,
wondrous and awesome. So that's when
we had a name that we could call
these beasts, thanks to Richard Owen.

Owen was born in Lancaster:
we think that when he was at school
his attitude caused quite a stir
for not adhering to the rules,

and this is something, you might say,
continued throughout his whole life
with colleagues, peers; he had a way
of causing upset, grudge and strife.

But he had skill, and when he'd see
some bones dug up from ground, or pit,
Comparative Anatomy
meant he could see how they might fit

together; he knew how to build
the skeletons from tooth to claw,
and dreamed of a museum, filled
with bones and fossils, roof to floor

that could be seen by anyone:
not just the top-hat-wearing rich,
but *all* who want to gaze upon
these creatures, raised from rock and ditch,

so all of us could understand
and have the chance to come to know
about the beasts that roamed our land
two hundred million years ago.

He may have caused controversy
but still, he opened up the doors
to halls of natural history,
and why we call them dinosaurs.

Known until recently as 'the British
Museum (Natural History)', the
Natural History Museum in South
Kensington was Richard Owen's
crowning achievement.

Take a look at Lorraine
Mariner's poem on page
14 for another glance at
the museum.

THE BONE WARS

Philip Monks

There were two American men
who lived in the Victorian way-back-when.
They loved their fossils and both went out to the desert
   and got them,
but they also hated each other something rotten.

Othniel Charles Marsh
was deliberately harsh
to his rival Mr. Cope,
and often lied about him, or, as he put it, 'mis-spoke.'

Edward Drinker Cope
thought that if he gave enough rope
To Mr. Marsh's devious plots
He would tie himself in knots.

They lied and cheated and worse –
their fossil mania a curse
that made each of them want to crush
the other's discoveries to dust.

They fought a lot
over the dinosaur bones they'd got,
and what their discoveries said
about the lives the prehistoric creatures led.

Their collecting went on and on and only stopped
when the fossil-hunting dinosaur expeditionary bubble
    finally popped.
Then, with their money all gone,
they just couldn't carry on.

So Mr. Marsh and Mr. Cope
ended up angry, twisted, bitter and broke
because they started a dinosaur bone war –
a cautionary story of taking finding things too far.

However: although we do still mind that they were unkind,
they left behind such amazing finds
that perhaps it's enough to remember them as clever,
    ruthless, rough and tough,
since we now have all their fantastic dinosaur stuff.

Before Marsh and Cope,
we only knew about a few
kinds of dinosaurs — mostly
ones from Europe.

Powered by their intense hatred
for each other, the two uncovered
some of the most famous Mesozoic
animals, including *Brontosaurus*,
Elasmosaurus, and *Stegosaurus*.

But they worked so
hurriedly and so angrily
that some of the mess they
made is still being sorted
out by scientists!

If you want to improve
palaeontology, it's better to be
good at teamwork, hanging
out, and being buddies.

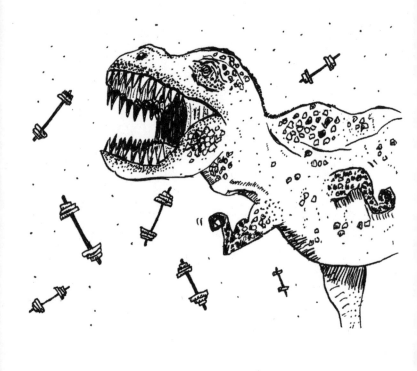

HEAVYWEIGHT CHAMP

Lawrence Schimel

One dinosaur did pushups
because his arms were thin.
He practiced night and day –
such steadfast discipline!

He very soon developed
bulging arms and pecs.
The other dinos called him
Tyrannosaurus Flex.

ROAR, ROAR, T. REX

Myles McLeod

Roar, roar, T. rex
Have you had your lunch?

Yes sir, yes sir,
Crunch crunch crunch.

One ceratopsid,
One pterosaur,
And sorry to inform you
I still have room for more!

Roar, roar, T. rex
Have you had your lunch?

Yes sir, yes sir,
Crunch crunch crunch.

T. rex is famously thought to have preyed on *Triceratops*, the most well-known of the ceratopsians.

Some have theorised that *Tyrannosaurus* was a scavenger rather than an active predator, though most now believe that *T. rex* hunted its food. Whichever theory is correct, it was probably best not to get too close.

MARY ANNING ROARS TO THE SEA

Sophie Kirtley

*In 1811, twelve year old Mary Anning found
the first complete Ichthyosaur skeleton on the
beach near her home in Lyme Regis.*

Wild waves crash, raw winds roar:
I hear the voice of the lost dinosaur.
I roar back. I am bold.
I roar because in my hand I hold
my hammer
to break
these rocks
apart
and unlock the secrets
at their old, cold heart.

'I found your bones!'
I shout, all alone,
to the plesiosaur
who paddled and dived
who lived, then died,
right here, before,
so long before

me,

in my wind-flapped gown
with my salt-wet hair
staring down at the ground,
then up
up at the fast grey sky,
where seven white gulls
circle and cry, and circle, and I
squeeze my eyes half shut
and I half-spy

a pterosaur
on the wing.
'I found your bones!'
I roar to the thing
who isn't really there
anymore, then I roar
as I sing a half-made song,
with words half-right
and words half-wrong
with wild words lost
in the wind-spun air
and why do I sing?

Because I dare.

I dare to dig,
and I dare
to find

the bones and the shadows
left behind.
I dare to turn stone after stone
after stone,
I wear hard boots
and I walk all alone,
here, right here,
with my hammer in my hand,
I dare to walk the land-slipped
shifty sand,
and I dare to learn
and to understand.

I dare to sing and I dare to roar
like the dinosaurs
who dared here
long long
before.

Plesiosaurs and
ichthyosaurs, though they
also lived in the Mesozoic,
are technically marine
mammals rather than
dinosaurs.

Also, as you might
remember from John
Canfield's poem on page
47, this poem takes place
thirty years before the
word dinosaur was even
invented!

THE TERROR-DRAGON'S THIGHBONE

Gita Ralleigh

after the fall of the three kingdoms,
after the time of magician-emperors
who transformed to birds when they died.
in a time rich in bronze, jade and gold,

in our land between mountains and seas.
rice, peaches, silk, good things flourished.
we did not need oracle bones to tell
which way the wind was blowing,

spreading the fires of rebellion.
digging the field, my spade rang upon
a buried thing: hard but not stone,
long but not a rusted plough-tool,

caked in wet earth, a bone wide as
a young tree-trunk. I poured water upon it,
rubbed rough ivory with my sleeve,
prayed to the powerful emperor of

all creatures: oh terror-dragon, whose
stoneground bones cure sickness,
forgive me, poor yet blessed with children.
heaping yellow earth over the dragon's

thighbone, I bent once more to digging.
later that night by a lit moon, rolling
through cloud like a silver coin worn thin,
later I returned to claim it for my own.

During the Western Jin Dynasty (265-316 AD), the historian Chang Qu wrote in his book *Hua Yang Guo Zhi* about the discovery of dragon bones in Sichuan.

More recently, villagers in central China showed researchers some 'dragon-bones' used for medicine that turned out to be dinosaur fossils.

PALAEONTOLOGIST

Jane Newberry

I wish I was a scientist
investigating bones
in some museum laboratory,
away from sport and phones.

With bits of real fossil,
I'd brush off all the grime,
then digitally log them
in their prehistoric time.

I'd fly to distant deserts
and, lifting up the floor,
I'd dig down twenty feet to find
a real raptor claw!

I know I could be useful;
I've read papers, blogs and books
on the Mesozoic era
and how Baryonyx looks.

But school thinks you need numeracy
and stuff like PSE,
which, as a palaeontologist
is not much good to me.

Both numeracy and PSE are incredibly useful to palaeontologists, of course – without numeracy, there's no investigating the age of rocks, the populations of animals, or the way their bodies would have moved.

As for PSE: dinosaur reproduction is still a matter of serious discussion among experts. How do you think giant sauropods had babies?

DIPLODOCUS

Bo Crowder

We are the dinosaurs who have the longest nose to tail-ucus
Our reach for leaves and branches in the trees can never fail-ucus
Our brains are very small and very far from intellectual-us
We cannot sing at all and if we dance it's ineffectual-us
We have no fashion sense and like our colour to be bland-ulus
We don't do skinny anything because our size is grand-ulus
Magnificent and odd-icus the greatest sauropod-icus
Stupendously named twice as dip-lo-docus and dip-lodicus.

We lumber in the mountains and we stumble on the trail-ucus
We've sunken all the boats and ships we ever tried to sail-ucus
There never was a game we ever mastered with a ball-ucus
We're far too proud to try and pride comes first before a fall-ucus
We're perfectly proportioned in our eyes we pass the test-ulus
Of all the beasts you've ever seen surely we are the best-ulus
The great Jurassic God-icus the finest sauropod-icus
Stupendously named twice as dip-lo-docus and dip-lodicus.

The 'diplo' in *Diplodocus* means 'double', so the final line of each verse here is doubly appropriate! This dinosaur was given its tricky-to-pronounce name by Othniel Marsh (see Phil Monks's poem on page 49) in 1878.

WHAT DID DINOSAURS SMELL LIKE?

Louise Crosby

I am sure they were not scented
like soap, deodorant
or lily flowers.

And certainly not sweet,
like candy floss, doughnuts,
sticky bonfire toffee.

Nor savoury
like chicken crisps, blue cheese
or onion gravy.

Not even mechanical:
racing cars, petrol pumps
or tumble dryers.

But dinosaur smell
was, surely,
somewhere between

egg sandwiches,
raw burgers,
and farmyards.

COMPLAINT OF THE SPINOSAURUS

Kate Wise

Mu-um!
Please don't make me have swimming lessons.
I don't *care* that I've got webbed toes –
or that my nostrils are on top of my head.
The water still goes up my nose.
I get wrinkly by the end, and I'm *lonely*;
I'm the only dinosaur that swims;
the others at classes are true marine reptiles,
with flippers and scales and fins.

It doesn't matter that I'm bigger than T. rex,
he's laughing at me with my friends.
The others can already dive hundreds of feet!
I hope they end up with the bends.
My hat makes me look stupid;
my crest won't change colour when I'm blue with cold.
The teacher says that I'm a wimp
and I *don't* want to do what I'm told.

Mum. Please don't make me go swimming.
I don't even *like* the taste of squid.
It's really a waste of your money
– they cost you fifty quid.

Mum – I'll take up another hobby, promise.
I'll do anything you please:
the violin? Judo? A second language?
I reckon I could be good at Japanese...?

Those other swimming things
– icthyosaurs, mosasaurs, and
the like – weren't technically
part of the dinosaur family. But
Spinosaurus, a huge theropod
from North Africa, seems to
have enjoyed fishing.

Spinosaurus was named in
1915, but the first specimen
was destroyed by Allied
bombing during the Second
World War and it wasn't until
the 1990s that another one
was found.

THE DREADED DREADNOUGHTUS

B. J. Lee

We played in the forest
of Gondwana-Horus.
We sought the Dreadnoughtus,
the titanosaurus.

With swagger and haught-us,
we sought the Dreadnoughtus.
With swords for the onslaught,
we sought the Dreadnoughtus.

We saw the Dreadnoughtus,
that horrid old saurus.
He stood in the forest.
Ah! How he awed us!

He turned and he saw us.
He didn't care for us.
He made a great roar-us.
We screamed in a chorus.

We ran lest he paw us
or claw us or gnaw us.
We ran through the forest
of Gondwana-Horus.

We outran the saurus,
relieved to the core-us!
We beat the Dreadnoughtus,
that naughty old saurus.

But Dreadnoughtus taught us
to not be so haught-us,
or play in the forest
of Gondwana-Horus.

Gondwana was one of the
two continents which were
slowly breaking into our
current world map during
the time of the dinosaurs.

It gradually became Africa,
South America, Australia,
Antarctica, and India. The
other continent – now
Europe, North America, and
Asia – was called Laurasia.

PTHE PTERANODON

Pete Donald

Pthink of flying dinosaurs,
pthat filled prehistoric skies.
Pthe greatest pterror of pthem all,
with large fish-seeking eyes.

A very intelligent reptile,
with a wingspan over ptwenty feet.
Let's hear it for pthe Pteranodon.
Just pto see one would be a ptreat.

MR BONES

Jane Burn

Barnum was a fossil-finder, fossil-finder, sure!
Digger, hunter, duster, blaster – had bones to procure!
Sailed a boat called *Mary Jane*, filled up trains: busy man!
Barnum Brown the fossil-finder, finding all he can!

He loved these buried treasures. He got to know them well –
as a child he had collections of prehistoric shells.
Scouring rock and sediment, he brought the past before us,
dredged the dirt of Hell Creek to reveal *Tyrannosaurus*

rex. The first one ever seen! Albertosaurus feet –
skeletons, great skeletons, both scattered and complete!
Fossil-finder excavating Mesozoic life –
I married a dinosaur said his fossil-finding wife.

Lilian MacLaughlin Brown, also
known as Pixie, was Barnum
Brown's second wife. As well as
I Married a Dinosaur, she wrote
another book of her adventures
with her husband called *Bring
'Em Back Petrified.*

The rules of science prevent a dinosaur from having two different official names.

In the confusion of the Bone Wars (see Phil Monks's poem on page 49), Othniel Marsh named both *Brontosaurus* and *Apatosaurus* – but it was later discovered that these were the same animal, and *Apatosaurus* was the older name. First come, first served!

This meant that *Brontosaurus* – 'thunder lizard' – wasn't used as the technical term for the entire twentieth century.

In 2015, Emanuel Tschopp, Octávio Mateus, and Roger Benson suggested that *Brontosaurus* might be different enough from *Apatosaurus* to be allowed its name back.

BRONTOSAURUS BACKLASH

Jane Frank

I wondered where you went,
Brontosaurus –
swamp loving behemoth,
cedar-tailed thunder lizard
of the late Jurassic.
I admired your long neck,
your 80-foot extravagance,
the way you made the ground shake.
You were the dearest prize in the Cornflakes packet.
I won a competition with a felt pen
drawing of you swimming with
prehistoric fish and pterodactyls in the sky.

Then one day I read in the paper
you were a casualty of the 'Bone Wars' –
written off as an *Apatosaurus ajax* for decades,
lost in a different type of extinction.
That was, of course, until Stephen Jay Gould
announced it was all a 'tempest in a teapot' –
and other scientists re-found you too,
albeit changing your personality somewhat.

You now ground ferns in your gizzards,
had moved from lake to land,
from a plodder to a mover and shaker –
maybe even a dub stepper.
You stood on your rear legs now
to reach high plants and impress your mates.
You had 'incredible allure' according to
Emanuel Tschopp who checked your fossils
and declared, without hesitation,
that you undoubtedly had a
survivor's sting in your tail.

66 MILLION YEARS

Ros Woolner

A lifetime, when you're six like Jane,
is just six years.
Jane's grandma on her mother's side
is sixty-six
(eleven times Jane's age) and when
Jane goes to school
she learns about the olden days:
sixteen sixty-six,
a fire in London. Further back:
ten sixty-six,
a famous battle down in Hastings.
But this T. rex
lived millions of years ago:
sixty-six million.
Jane can't imagine that much time.
Six zeros. Wow!
The number's huge, like T. rex here,
who weighed six tonnes
though now he's just a skeleton
of fossils –
three hundred (six times fifty) bones,
some real, some fake,

twelve metres long (two lots of six)
from teeth to tail.

How many six-year-olds, asks Jane,
could T. rex eat?

The *Iliad*, pretty much the oldest work of
Western literature, is around 2,800 years
old. The Chicxulub asteroid, meanwhile,
ended the time of the non-bird dinosaurs
around 66 million years ago.

In order to get from today to the last living
T. rex, then, you would need to walk the
length of human civilisation 23,500 times.

But that's just the most recent dinosaurs!
T. rex's ancestors arose in the Triassic,
another 177 million years before *that*.
More time separates the first non-bird
dinosaur from the last than separates the
last from our puny civilisation.

THIS IS HOW WE WALKED

Jane Burn

T
h
i
s
is
how
we
walked,
all those
years ago –
those hundreds,
thousands and
millions of years
that we spent,
pressing ourselves
to the mud. Into
sand and seabed,
forest floor and
mountain side.
We ran on two
or sometimes
four legs, swam
or flew. Paddled,
dabbled, were

e
x
p
e
r
im
ent
al.
Were
a practise
run. Were
evolution. Some
of us were fast,
some of us slow.
No matter – we
almost mostly
got there in the end.
Plod or gallop,
go lightly or
galumph, we lived
for a while as giants,
grand as pianos,
big as buses,
broad as vans.

M
e
a
s
ur
ing
our
steps
can
tell you our
speed or weight but
not the colour
of the moon
above as we
surrendered
ourselves to
the silt.
Some
secrets we
have
k
e
p
t.

You have learned the size of
our throats but not the
sound of our songs.

Bones aren't the only things
which fossilise! If you're lucky,
you could also find a trace fossil
— a footprint, coprolite, or other
mark left on the world by a
creature whose other remains
have been lost.

A poem which looks like the
thing it describes is called a
'concrete poem'. One of the
earliest was written by Simmias
of Rhodes in about 300BCE.

Since he died millennia ago
and the location of his body is
unknown, in a way Simmias's
poetry is a trace fossil — a hint
at an otherwise unknowable life
— as the poem on the opposite
page may one day also be.

AT THE DINOSAUR MUSEUM

Daniel Leonard

Come right through the double doors
for one of our finest features!
We dinosaurs have ample stores
of time's forgotten creatures.

This specimen's a trilobite,
an early arthropod.
Compared to us, it's small and light –
and doesn't it look odd?

In oceans of the Paleozoic
they waded waves worldwide.
I call that humble work heroic,
as your finely-feathered guide.

In life, this layered oval shell
paraded with its peers.
Their twenty thousand kinds did well
for a quarter billion years.

We don't know how the tide was turned
to leave them cold and docile.
There's still plenty to be learned
from this exquisite fossil.

What beasts now fully lost to time
did galleries display
to curious trilobites in their prime?
Who alive can say?

In sour days for dinosaurs
will we too earn admissions
with front-row seats for guided tours
of extinction exhibitions?

Could future races think us strange?
What would they be like?
Will beings feel even then how change
awaits its chance to strike?

When earth consumes its final friend,
who will come to see him?
Will there ever be an end
of ending up museumed?

That's all the time we have today!
The doors are about to close.
It's gotten late. Go home and play
with the souvenirs you chose.

TO THE LAST DINOSAUR STANDING

Kate Wakeling

Because there had to be *one*, who watched the world sizzle and crack as it faced that almighty asteroid THWACK (if we're sure this is the fixture that finished them off). There had to be one who saw skies thicken with black, who watched the wilt of every shred of green, who trod through dust to seek a last curled leaf, or gnawed upon some final bit of dino-beef. And it must have been a horrible happening, that sink from life, that sudden stop to the business of being a dinosaur (I suspect). And so I hail the beast whose heart ticked on this extra hour, who sighed and stood alone upon the ruined ground before it took its endmost gulp. I salute you, whichever cool-blooded soul it was who came to be the last to go, whose tiny walnut brain must have meant (I only hope) that of its lonely fate, it could not know.

See Rebecca Rouillard's poem on page 42 for another animal facing the horror of the asteroid...

FOWL DREAMS

Marilyn Anne Campbell

If you gave a thought to chicken dreams,
you might presume them meek –
dreams of bugs and grubs and beetles ample,
and perfect garden beds to trample.
Or maybe you would grant these birds
a little more mystique –
and imagine dreams filled with warm air thermals,
lifting them in drifting circles.
Oh, you might think a chicken
dreams of these things –
of tasty meals or broad, strong wings.

But I have watched a sleeping chicken
twitch its claws, its breathing quicken –
and I don't believe chickens dream of soaring...

No, chicken dreams are filled with roaring!
In the night they travel back
over 60 million years –
they trade their beaks for dagger teeth.
They tower and glower at other beasts.
They crash through giant redwoods
as the coop life disappears.

After all, why should they care for farm or flock
when their dream-claws can gouge scars in rock?
Yes, at night chickens are predators, no longer prey.

That's what happens when there's T. rex in your DNA.

THE END

Marilyn Anne Campbell

Should I give the thumbs up
or the 'A-OK' sign
as I sink into the tar?

I want the discovery to be colossal
when future generations uncover my fossil.

Tar is a great way of preserving fossils!
One of the most famous fossil sites in the
world is the La Brea tar pits in California,
although these contain Pleistocene
mammals (such as sabretooth tigers and
mammoths) rather than dinosaurs.

AFTER THE ASTEROID

Jeremy Wikeley

After the asteroid there was nothing.
There was so much nothing
it was as if there had never been anything.

No leaf things. No T. rex things.
No leathery things or feathery things.
No things with fins. Nothing.

After the asteroid there was nothing.
You say I'm repeating myself?
I'm going to say it again. For a moment

there was everything. T. rex things.
Finny things. Leafy things. And in a moment
all those things were nothing.

It was as if there had never been anything.
After the asteroid there was nothing
except a tiny long-nosed furry thing

and another tiny long-nosed furry thing.
You say I'm contradicting myself?
I'm going to say it again. There was nothing

except two tiny long-nosed furry things
hiding beneath the ground and poking
their long furry noses up out into nothing.

Then, later, you and me things.

Mammals – the group of creatures
which now includes you – emerged
in the Triassic Period, like dinosaurs.
They tended to be small, about
mouse-sized, when they had
dinosaurs to compete with – in fact,
the majority of mammal species are
still very tiny to this day!

After the Chicxulub asteroid, mammals
diversified very successfully and – in
a few cases – were able to get bigger.
This has eventually led to us, but also,
more importantly, to echidnas (which
are cooler than us).

BONUS BITS

INTERVIEW WITH A PALAEONTOLOGIST

What's it actually like to be a palaeontologist, working with dinosaurs every day? We asked Dr Shaena Montanari...

What made you want to be a palaeontologist?

Growing up, I was just so fond of all animals and nature. I loved walking on the beach and collecting seashells, catching frogs in the stream, and reading about wildlife from around the world. I also had a great rock collection!

 I realized palaeontology was a way I could combine my love of the Earth with my curiosity about animals. Palaeontology is the perfect way to combine many sciences all into one very interesting package.

What does a typical day at work look like?

A typical day for a palaeontologist is generally not as exciting as it may seem in the movies! In the office, which in my experience is the majority of the time, we mostly write and work on describing our finds so other scientists can learn about them, or have meetings. Of course, if you're lucky, a few weeks or months out of the year involve fieldwork where you collect fossils and data that you can work on the rest of the year. A lot of palaeontologists also teach classes and have students, so there is always a lot going on.

What's the coolest thing you've ever found?

The first time I went to Mongolia, I found half of a fossil bird egg with tiny bones in it. It was just so incredible to me that this unhatched bird stayed intact for 75 million years and then I found it!

Do you have a favourite dinosaur?

I would say my favorite dinosaur is *Velociraptor*. They are small and mighty, and are found in Mongolia, which is the first place I did palaeontology fieldwork.

What would you recommend to a young person interested in becoming a palaeontologist?

Visit as many museums as you can! They are the best places to learn more about fossils and science in general. If you are able, travel around and find places to dig up fossils for fun to see what it is like – you might not even realize it, but there could be fossil localities near your own house. It is worth researching online to see what you can find.

Also, make sure you study all sorts of science in school – chemistry, physics, biology, and geology – because all of them can be used in the study of palaeontology.

Dr Shaena Montanari received her PhD in comparative biology from the Richard Gilder Graduate School at the American Museum of Natural History in New York.

Her dissertation was on the palaeoecology of dinosaurs and mammals, which led her to field work in Mongolia's Gobi Desert and the outback of Australia. Her undergraduate degree in geological sciences was at the University of North Carolina Chapel Hill.

WRITE YOUR OWN POEM

Fancy writing your own poem and then maybe illustrating it too? Editor **Richard O'Brien** has come up with some ideas to help you get started.

DINO DIALOGUE

No one living today has ever heard a dinosaur roar – in fact, some scientists now think it's more likely that they growled like crocodiles, or even honked like geese. In any case, they definitely didn't talk like humans. But lots of the poets in this book have imagined voices for dinosaurs, like Lawrence Schimel's 'Heavyweight Champ' (page 53) or Lesley Sharpe's 'Formerly Mr Iguanodon' (page 36).

When we imagine dinosaurs today, we often think of them all living side-by-side, even though some familiar species evolved millions of years apart. One amazing fact is that we are closer in time to *T. rex* than *T. rex* lived to *Stegosaurus*. But as poets, of course, we can imagine the impossible!

Looking across the whole book, **pick out two dinosaurs from different poems (or a favourite of yours that isn't featured here) and write a conversation between them.**

The most important thing is to give them two very different voices. A big dinosaur like *Dreadnoughtus* might speak in a BIG VOICE, WITH ALL CAPITALS, or be slow and only use short words.

A little one, like a *Velociraptor* or the 'tiny' *Junornis huoi* (page 6) might have smaller writing, or be able to dart around very quickly and be nimble with its language. They might be talking about normal dinosaur topics, or about their favourite lessons at school – the subject is up to you. If you want, you could have their conversation be a series of questions and answers.

WHAT I WAS REALLY LIKE

We know that scientists have sometimes got the position of dinosaurs' bones mixed up, or not noticed that some dinosaurs had feathers, or thought they were more mean and fierce than they actually were.

Pick a dinosaur who you think might have been misunderstood in this way. Your poem is going to be your dinosaur having their own chance to speak, with the title 'What I was really like.' If it's helpful, you can use two phrases to help structure your poem:

'You think', e.g. 'You think I'm scary...' / 'You think I fought...' / 'You think I ate...' etc

'But you don't know...' e.g. 'you don't know that I was a good friend to other dinosaurs' – and explain how you were good in your life: what did you do?

We're thinking about using contrast in our writing, and the different ways to tell a story: there is a big difference between thinking and knowing, and often scientists – as well as writers – just have to guess on the best available evidence!

'HOW TO BE...'

Jon Stone's two poems, 'How to Be a Fused Lizard' (page 44) and 'How to Be a Spiked Lizard' (page 46), give a series of instructions on what you would need to do to make your body look like these particular types of dinosaur.

Some of the language is quite close to real life and some is a bit more fanciful, imagining how someone's emotions might be shown in physical form. The poems work as instructions because they use imperative verbs: the forms of verbs that you use to tell other people what to do, like 'Stand up straight' or 'Tidy your room'.

Think of a particular type of dinosaur and then write your own list of instructions that would help a person to turn into one: if you're writing about *Triceratops*, for instance, you could start with 'Grow three horns from the top of your head', unless the person you're imagining already has one or two horns of their own!

The majority of your poem should be lines using these imperative verbs, but as you get towards the end you might want to do what Jon does and also think about the consequences of these kinds of physical appearance.

Because *Kentrosaurus* is so sharp and pointy, other dinosaurs 'learn to steer clear' of it: what would happen to a person who became the kind of dinosaur you're thinking of? Do you want to warn them about potential reactions – or tell them what they have to look forward to?

INTERVIEW-A-SAURUS

Some of the poems in this book are about asking dinosaurs the big questions: like 'Just how big is a dinosaur egg?' (page 30), 'What did dinosaurs smell like?' (page 66) or 'How many six-year-olds could T. rex eat?' (on page 78). But it's very likely that you have questions of your own that haven't yet been raised.

Write a poem where you list all the questions you have about a dinosaur's life, either addressed to that specific dinosaur or asking rhetorical questions, where the point is partly that no one can ever know the answer.

Look at Helen Clare's poem on page 30 for a good example of this, and of how to keep a poem varied even though every line is a question, by using different lengths of line and strings of rhyming words. Could you try to do something similar?

TWO TIMES

In Valerie Valente's poem 'Wing Finger' (page 16), the speaker goes back and forth between describing the bones of a *Pterodactylus* on display in a museum, and imagining what it would be like if it was alive. Valerie uses **the past tense** for the bones – 'he **was** laid neatly in a case' – and the conditional for her fantasy of the creature flying: 'His bat-like wings **would** stretch so wide as he glided.'

Try using two different tenses like this in your own writing about a dinosaur, to switch between describing the fossil and describing the living animal.

PALEO POEMS

Rachael Nicholas, John Canfield, and Philip Monks are some of the poets in this book who have written poems about specific palaeontologists whose dino discoveries helped us to get a better understanding of these long-ago creatures in the present day. To write these poems, they all had to do some research to find out the facts of their subjects' lives, and then re-tell them in an interesting way.

Perhaps with a parent or teacher's help, see if you can find the life story of a particular palaeontologist (dinosaur scientist), online or in your school library. Make some notes on what was interesting about their life, and think about how to choose the parts of the story that are most fun, or impressive, or surprising, to turn the raw facts of what they did into something that is engaging and memorable as a poetic retelling.

You might find it especially useful to think about what you're going to leave out – how you will jump ahead from one part of the story to the next. Do you want to leave the reader with some sense of mystery, or give them as many questions as answers? How will you separate the parts of the story into different verses and images?

REWRITE A RHYME

Myles McLeod's poem on page 54 uses the structure (and the tune!) of the famous nursery rhyme 'Baa Baa Black Sheep', but changes the words to relate to *T. rex*. It works well because there is something familiar to hang onto from the original rhyme, so you know how to sing it and the joke comes from the big differences between a sheep and a *T. rex* (at least, I hope you've noticed that there are some...) Try rewriting a famous nursery rhyme or song that you know – something like 'Humpty Dumpty' or 'Three Blind Mice' – to be about a dinosaur instead. The more you can push the difference between the original subject and the new dinosaur theme, the funnier it will be!

MAMMAL MONOLOGUE

On page 89, Jeremy Wikeley writes about the 'tiny long-nosed furry things' that shared the earth with dinosaurs – some mammals were actually much bigger than this at the time, but in any case, these mostly nocturnal creatures were the distant ancestors of our own species.

What did they think, looking up at all these great big dinosaurs stomping around? Were they scared, or just annoyed at them getting in the way? In whatever form you choose, write a poem from the perspective of a mammal living at the same time as the dinosaurs, giving your unique mammal insights on the whole scene as you see it from your level, much closer to the ground!

GROUP POEM: SKELETON

This is a writing exercise you might want to do with your school class, or with other people at home. Your group can create a dinosaur together by describing different bits of its skeleton: the idea is that every child writes about a different bone.

Imagine we've just uncovered a dinosaur skeleton, right here in your town.

Pick a part of this skeleton – head, jaw, ribs, feet, tail – and draw a big outline of it on a piece of paper. For best results, you should all pick a different part!

Now imagine you're a palaeontologist: describe what this bone looks like and what you can tell or guess about the dinosaur just by looking at it. How did it live? What did it eat, how did it move? Write some sentences inside your outline – try to use comparisons, like 'its teeth were as sharp as ....' or 'its leg-bone was as long as ....'

Stick this sheet on the wall next to other people who have done the same thing, and you can work out what kind of dinosaur you have found together! Why not give it a name that represents the people who discovered it: if you are the Butterfly Class, for example, it could be 'Butterfly-a-saurus'!

WHO MADE THIS BOOK?

HERE'S THE EDITOR, WHO CHOSE ALL THE POEMS IN THIS BOOK

Richard O'Brien is a poet, academic and translator based in Birmingham. He has co-translated three books of children's poetry from other languages for the Emma Press: *The Noisy Classroom* (Ieva Flamingo), *The Book of Clouds* (Juris Kronbergs), and *Everyone's the Smartest* (Contra). In 2017, he won an Eric Gregory Award from the Society of Authors for his own poetry for adults, and in 2018 he was appointed Birmingham Poet Laureate for two years. As a kid he once wrote to TV's Tony Robinson with his own personal theory about the extinction of the dinosaurs, but scientists as a whole remained unconvinced.

HERE'S WILL, WHO WROTE THE NOTES

Dr Will Tattersdill is a writer and teacher in the British higher education system. He is especially interested in how literature and science talk to each other, and has written about X-rays, future prediction, arctic exploration, and messages from Mars in addition to his current work on palaeontology. Though he currently has no dinosaurs – just a dog, a cat, and a rabbit – he dreams of having chickens one day.

HERE'S THE ILLUSTRATOR

Emma Dai'an Wright is a British-Vietnamese publisher, designer and illustrator based in Birmingham, UK. She worked in ebook production at Orion Publishing Group before leaving in 2012 to set up the Emma Press with the support of the Prince's Trust. She has since published over 500 writers across more than 60 books, including poetry anthologies for adults and children, short stories, and translations.

AND HERE ARE ALL THE POETS!

Jane Burn is a poet that loves anything old. Especially if it is dusty and has to be dug from the ground. She pretends to be an archaeologist who specialises in finding bits of broken pottery and historical bottles.

Marilyn Anne Campbell lives in Toronto, Canada with her partner Steve and their many cats. She likes to be outside with the birds or inside the Royal Ontario Museum, where she always says hello to the *Futalognkosaurus* in the lobby. Someday, Marilyn hopes to read one of your poems in a book.

John Canfield grew up in Cornwall and now tries not to be a grown up in London. He writes poems and sometimes people put them in books and sometimes they don't. He has ginger hair, like a *Sinosauropteryx*.

Helen Clare used to be a science teacher and she still likes to mix science with poetry and art, and enjoys working with schools, community groups and museums. Her publications include *Mollusc* (Comma 2004) and *Entomology* (2014)

Louise Crosby is an illustrator, poet and teacher. She illustrates poems as comics in a project called Seeing Poetry. She is learning to write without pictures and has a poem in *Watermarks Anthology*, published by Bluemoose Books. She delivers comics workshops and runs Laydeez do Comics, Leeds.

Bo Crowder comes from a working-class community dominated by heavy industry. His debut collection, *Euphony*, was published by Offa's Press in 2016. He regularly performs at poetry readings and is a founder member of the Staffordshire Poetry Stanza.

Pete Donald is a children's story writer and storyteller from Newcastle upon Tyne. He was shortlisted for the 2017 National Literacy Trust short story for 'What's in a Name'. He also volunteers for Live Tales and Beanstalk and is the chairman of the SSWAG children's writing group in Newcastle.

Jane Frank is an Australian poet who teaches creative writing and literary studies at Griffith University. Recent poems have appeared in *Algebra of Owls, Not Very Quiet* and *Pale Fire: New Writings on the Moon* (Frogmore Press, 2019). She loves reading scary dinosaur stories to her young sons Euan and Alastair.

Camille Gagnier's dad raised her on discussions about Homer, the mourning families of roadkill, and weird critters of the precambrian explosion. She is a graduate of the Great Books Program at St. John's College, and will be studying for a postgraduate degree in philosophy in 2018.

Wye Haze lives in London and writes poems for adults and children, though often can't tell which are for which. She used to hide all her poems in a box under the bed but one day the lid burst off. Her favourite character in 'The Land Before Time' is Cera.

Sophie Kirtley hatched in Northern Ireland and now does most of her stomping in South West England. She's just graduated with Distinction from the MA in Writing for Young Sauropods at Bath Spa Dinoversity. Sophie's poems and stories have won prizes in *Mslexia, Writing Magazine* and *The Caterpillar*. If you ever meet Sophie, don't worry – she's a herbivore.

John Kitchen used to teach projects like dinosaurs and now he writes about them. He's enjoyed doing both.

B.J. Lee's poems have appeared in anthologies including *Construction People* (ed. Lee Bennett Hopkins), *The National Geographic Book of Nature Poetry* and *The Poetry of US* (ed. J. Patrick Lewis), *One Minute Till Bedtime* (ed. Kenn Nesbitt), and others. Her debut picture book is forthcoming from Pelican.

Daniel Leonard is an American poet and teacher. This is his first time writing about animals for children. Next he hopes to write about children for animals. His favorite dinosaurs are the sauropods, because their necks soar up oddly.

Harry Man, a bipedal hominid from the Holocene, lives in Middlesbrough. His first pamphlet, *Lift* (Tall Lighthouse) won the Bridges of Struga Award. His second pamphlet, *Finders Keepers* (Sidekick Books), a collaboration with artist Sophie Gainsley, was shortlisted for the Ted Hughes Award for New Work in Poetry.

Lorraine Mariner has published two poetry collections for adults with Picador. Her work with children at the National Poetry Library has inspired her to start writing children's poetry. Visiting the Natural History Museum, London, when she was four with her mum, dad and brother is one of her earliest memories.

Myles McLeod writes for children's TV and has written for Hey Duggee, Clangers, Noddy Toyland Detective and Octonauts. He also studied Palaeobiology at University. He once spent a week on the Yorkshire Coast looking for dinosaur tracks! Myles runs the Poetry Picture Club which features poems illustrated by Wilm Lindenblatt.

Emma Rose Millar is a mum, author and poet from Birmingham. Her novel *Delirium* was shortlisted for the Chanticleer Paranormal Novel Awards, and her novella *The Women Friends: Selina was* shortlisted for the Goethe Award for Historical Fiction. In her spare time, she loves swimming, yoga and making pretty things.

Philip Monks has published three poetry pamphlets and is a Postcard Poet for Poetry On Loan. He regularly runs creative writing projects in schools and has co-edited five anthologies of young people's writing. As Dr. Philip he is an Advanced Skills Tutor for The Brilliant Club. He lives in Bristol.

Jane Newberry spent over twenty years sharing music and rhyme with young children, parents, carers and grandparents. Jane has published two songbooks, *A Sackful of Songs* and *A Sackful of*

Christmas (Cramer Music). 2020 heralds Jane's first book of verse, *Tickle Beetle,* illustrated by Carolina Rabei (Otter Barry).

Rachael M Nicholas is a poet from Birmingham. In 2012 she was lucky enough to win the Eric Gregory Award. Some of her poems in previous Emma Press anthologies have been about space (very big!), the Minotaur (very scary!) and Ariadne (very, very clever!).

Valerie L. Pate was born in America but has lived in the UK for over a decade. Valerie has been a voracious writer since the age of nine, and poetry is her first and truest love. Valerie often finds herself writing about nature and wildlife. Her two young daughters are her greatest inspiration.

Cheryl Pearson lives and writes in Manchester. Her poems have appeared or are forthcoming in publications including the *Guardian, Southword, The High Window, Under The Radar* and *The Compass.* She has twice been nominated for a Pushcart Prize. Her first full poetry collection, *Oysterlight*, is available now.

Gita Ralleigh discovered poetry rather late, after studying medicine and working as a doctor. She thinks the way a poem can be small and very large at the same time is magic. She enjoys sharing her new enthusiasm, running a children's book group and teaching writing workshops for medical students.

Rebecca Rouillard has a Creative Writing degree from Birkbeck. Her writing has appeared in various online and print anthologies, most recently in *Watermarks: Writing by Lido Lovers and Wild Swimmers.* Her YA novel, *Ash & Ellyn and the Lighthouse,* won the 2017 Mslexia Novel Competition.

Lawrence Schimel was born in New York City and has lived in Madrid, Spain for almost 20 years. He writes in both Spanish and English. His poems appear in numerous other Emma Press collections, including *Watcher of the Skies* and *Slow Things.*

Lesley Sharpe teaches in London, and likes talking to dinosaurs on Sunday afternoons. She founded Poetry Garden to explore nature, literature and art with children and adults. Most recently her poems have been shortlisted for *The London Magazine*, *Aesthetica*, and Bridport Prizes.

Jon Stone is a writer and editor who specialises in hybrid forms, sequences and collaborations. He has co-edited and published a number of anthologies with Sidekick Books, including one on computer game poetry. He once kept a 'Dinosaur Denouement Diary' for a month – every entry ended with him being killed by a different dinosaur.

Kate Wakeling's debut collection of children's poetry, *Moon Juice* (Emma Press), won the 2017 CLiPPA. A pamphlet of her poetry for adults, *The Rainbow Faults*, is published by The Rialto. Kate continues to experience unexpectedly powerful emotional pangs on hearing the soundtrack to Jurassic Park.

Rob Walton writes poetry and very short stories, which he loves performing to children. His work has appeared in various magazines and anthologies. He follows Scunthorpe United, a team that once had a pterodactyl for a goalkeeper. Sometimes he can spell palaeontologist.

Cat Weatherill is a performance storyteller and author. She loves to travel the world and write in exotic coffee shops. She lives in a tiny black and white cottage that is four hundred years old and is allergic to cats. And gold.

Ruth Wiggins lives in London. Her poems have appeared most recently in *POETRY* and *Poetry Review*, and her pamphlet *Myrtle* was published by the Emma Press in 2014. Her goddaughters Hester and Niamh once had an enormous inflatable T. rex called Ruthie Rex. Her poem 'Tiny' is for them.

Jeremy Wikeley grew up in Romsey, near Southampton, where he regularly visited the (model) dinosaurs at Paultons Park. He now lives in London where he is regularly visits the (model) dinosaurs at Crystal Palace.

Kate Wise has been published in various Emma Press anthologies, and journals including the *Rialto, Structo* and *Poems in Which.* She has collected fossils from beaches around the country, but still isn't sure how to spell *Parasauropho... Parasauroloph...* the hooty one. She grew up in Cheshire, and tweets at @kwise62

Elli Woollard is not a dinosaur, although sometimes her children seem to think she is. The author of several critically acclaimed books, including *The Giant of Jum* (Macmillan), she lives in London with her family and her crazy cat. Other poems she has written are published by the Emma Press and Bloomsbury.

Ros Woolner lives in Wolverhampton with her family and a cat that loves sitting on paper. She helped translate '*T. rex* - MB.R.91216', the companion book to the 'Tristan – Berlin bares teeth' exhibition at the Natural History Museum in Berlin.

Finlay Worrallo grew up near London, where he fell in love with dinosaurs at the Natural History Museum. These days he lives in Yorkshire and likes travelling the world, learning foreign languages and making up stories. His favourite dinosaur is the *Stegosaurus.*

ABOUT THE EMMA PRESS

The Emma Press is an independent publishing house based in the Jewellery Quarter, Birmingham, UK. We specialise in poetry, short fiction and children's books.

The Emma Press won the Michael Marks Award for Poetry Pamphlet Publishers in 2016 and Emma Press books have won the Poetry Book Society Pamphlet Choice Award, the Saboteur Award for Best Collaborative Work, and CLiPPA, the CLPE award for children's poetry books.

We publish themed poetry anthologies, single-author poetry and fiction pamphlets (chapbooks), and books for children. We have a growing list of translations which includes titles from Latvia, Estonia, Indonesia, Spain and the Netherlands.

We run regular calls for submissions, and try to do as many events as possible, from book-launch parties to writing workshops to school visits.

You can find out more about the Emma Press and buy books directly from us here:

theemmapress.com

ALSO FROM THE EMMA PRESS

THE HEAD THAT WEARS A CROWN

Edited by Rachel Piercey and Emma Wright

Which King had a mischievous pet monkey? Which ruthless Queen enjoyed toasting people to a crisp? Whose reign lasted only nine days?

The Head That Wears A Crown is a captivating collection that features the kings and queens of the British Isles as you've never seen them before.

Intriguing, comical and accompanied by fascinating historical facts, these vibrant poems are a joy to read, bringing a long line of daring and devious monarchs to life.

£12.00
Paperback ISBN 978-1-910139-76-9
Poems aimed at children aged 8+

ALSO FROM THE EMMA PRESS

THE ADVENTURES OF NA WILLA

**Stories by Reda Gaudiamo, illustrated by Cecillia Hidayat
Translated from Indonesian by Ikhda Ayuning Maharsi
Degoul and Kate Wakeling**

Na Willa is a bright, adventurous girl living in Surabaya's suburbs, her home in the middle of an alley surrounded by cypress trees. She spends her days running after trains, going down to the market, and thinking about how people can sing through radios.

Reda Gaudiamo has created a collection of stories of curious adventures and musings of a multicultural girl growing up in Indonesia with an East Indonesian mother and a Chinese-Indonesian father.

£8.99

Paperback ISBN 978-1-910139-59-2
Stories aimed at children aged 8+

ALSO FROM THE EMMA PRESS

ONCE UPON A TIME IN BIRMINGHAM
WOMEN WHO DARED TO DREAM

Stories by Louise Palfreyman
Illustrations by Jan Bowman, Yasmin Bryan,
Amy Louise Evans, Saadia Hipkiss, Chein Shyan Lee,
Farah Osseili & Michelle Turton

Who was the world's first female programmer? Who
made history as the first British woman to sail solo around
the world non-stop? Who is Birmingham's first female
Muslim MP? Meet Mary Lee Berners-Lee, Lisa Clayton,
Shabana Mahmood and many more in *Once Upon a Time in
Birmingham*, a lively introduction to thirty of Birmingham's
most awe-inspiring women, past and present.

£14.99
Hardback ISBN 978-1-910139-82-0
Stories about real-life women aimed at children aged 11+

ALSO FROM THE EMMA PRESS

EVERYONE'S THE SMARTEST

Poems by Contra, illustrated by Ulla Saar
Translated from Estonian by Charlotte Geater,
Kätlin Kaldmaa & Richard O'Brien

School can be hard, fun and strange – sometimes all at once.
It's full of your best friends and all the teachers as well as lots
of kids you haven't met. Every day reveals more stories and
challenges... *Everyone's the Smartest* is a collection of poems
which tell strange new stories in familiar settings. From clever
ducks who fly far away while children are stuck in school, to
bathroom taps that are just one mistake away from turning the
school into a great lake, this collection reminds its readers that
there is wonder everywhere.

£12.00
Paperback ISBN 978-1-910139-99-8
Poems aimed at children aged 8+

ALSO FROM THE EMMA PRESS

THE BOOK OF CLOUDS

**Poems by Juris Kronbergs, illustrated by Anete Melece
Translated from Latvian by Mara Rozitis & Richard O'Brien.**

If you look up on a cloudy day, you'll see a whole new surprising world above you – the world of clouds! *The Book of Clouds* is an introduction to this world – and the guide you'll want by your side to help you understand it.

A mix of dreamy fantasy and scientific fact, this is the perfect gift for any child with their head stuck in the clouds – and for anyone who has ever wondered what's up there in the skies above. With 25 poems and many full-page illustrations that use watercolour and collage.

£12.00
Hardback ISBN 978-1-910139-14-1
Poems aimed at children aged 8+

ALSO FROM THE EMMA PRESS

THE DOG WHO FOUND SORROW

A story by Rūta Briede
Illustrated by Elīna Brasliņa
Translated from Latvian by Elīna Brasliņa

An entire city is suddenly enveloped in black clouds of sorrow that rob everything of colour and scent. A brave dog decides to resist the sadness and climbs up into the big cloud of sorrow to find out what's hiding up there – and to make it go away.

The Dog Who Found Sorrow is a poetic picture book for children and adults alike – a story about the power of emotions.

£10.00
Hardback ISBN 978-1-910139-54-7
A picture book aimed at children aged 4+

ALSO FROM THE EMMA PRESS

THE NOISY CLASSROOM

Poems by Ieva Samauska, illustrated by Vivianna Maria Staņislavska
Translated by Žanete Vēvere Pasqualini,
Sara Smith and Richard O'Brien

It isn't easy being a kid – especially not in the noisiest class in the school. Some days, you struggle with algebra, or too much homework. Sometimes, one of your fellow pupils just won't SHUT UP. *The Noisy Classroom* features poems which tackle social anxiety and the pressures of modern life on children, capturing familiar feelings of loneliness and being overworked. The book features bonus materials at the end. These give the reader an insight into the life of the writer and the illustrator, and encourage them to write and draw themselves.

£8.50
Hardback ISBN 978-1-910139-82-0
Poems aimed at children aged 8+

ALSO FROM THE EMMA PRESS

MOON JUICE

Poems by Kate Wakeling, illustrated by Elīna Brasliņa

Meet Skig, who's meant to be a warrior (but is really more of a worrier). Meet a giddy comet, skidding across the sky with her tail on fire. Put a marvellous new machine in your pocket and maybe you'll be able to fix all your life's problems.

Kate Wakeling's first book of poems for children is full of curious characters and strange situations. The poems she writes are always musical, sometimes magical, and full of wonder at the weirdness of the world.

Winner of the 2017 CLiPPA, the Centre of Literacy in Primary Education's award for children's poetry books

£8.50
Paperback ISBN 978-1-910139-49-3
Poems aimed at children aged 8+

ALSO FROM THE EMMA PRESS

QUEEN OF SEAGULLS

A picture book by Rūta Briede
Translated from Latvian by Elīna Brasliņa

Renata seems like an ordinary angry neighbour. She complains about children playing in the street, steals the food that people leave out for birds, and yells if she hears music. But there are things that Renata has forgotten about herself, and she must uncover the truth before it's too late...

What are the seagulls trying to tell her? And why do the accordionist's songs make her so cross? Will Renata ever remember who she really is? This is a story about seagulls, magic and true love.

£10.00
Hardback ISBN 978-1-910139-13-4
A picture book aimed at children aged 4+